# Sam

by Bobby Lynn Maslen
pictures by John R. Maslen

**Scholastic Inc.**
New York • Toronto • London • Auckland • Sydney • Mexico City • New Delhi • Hong Kong • Buenos Aires

# Beginning sounds for Book 2:

C c –  cat

D d –  dog

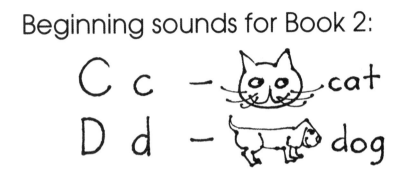

**Ask for Bob Books at your local bookstore, or visit www.bobbooks.com.**



ISBN 0-439-17546-1



12 11 10 13 14 15/0

Printed in China 68
This edition first printing, May 2006

Sam and Cat.

Mat and Cat.

Sam, Mat, and Cat.

Cat sat on Sam.

Mat sat on Sam.

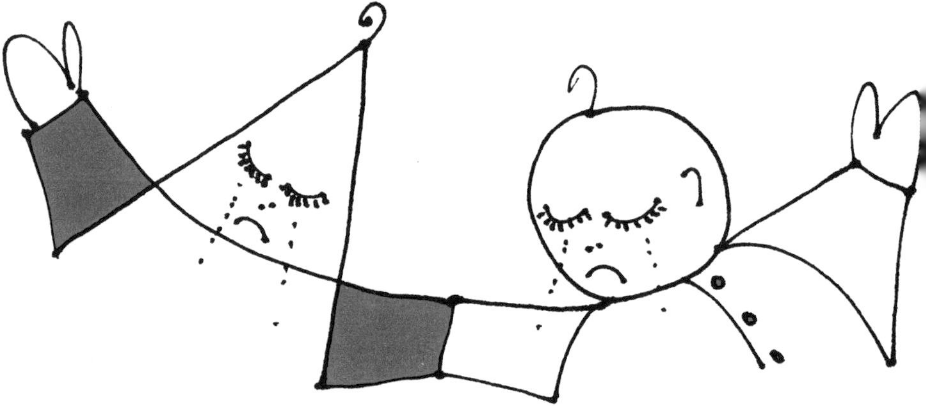

Sad Sam. Sad Mat.

Sam sat. Mat sat.

O.K., Sam. O.K., Mat. O.K., Cat.

# The End

**Available Bob Books®:**

Set 1: Beginning Readers

Set 2: Advancing Beginners

Set 3: Word Families

Set 4: Complex Words

Set 5: Long Vowels